In Shakespeare and the Bible

by Thornton Wilder

*This play became available through the
research and editing of F.J. O'Neil,
of manuscripts in the Thornton Wilder Collection
at Yale University.*

A SAMUEL FRENCH ACTING EDITION

SAMUELFRENCH.COM

FOR PRODUCTION ENQUIRIES

UNITED STATES AND CANADA
Info@SamuelFrench.com
1-866-598-8449

AMATEUR RIGHTS IN THE
UNITED KINGDOM
Plays@SamuelFrench-London.co.uk
020-7255-4302

Each title is subject to availability from Samuel French, depending upon country of performance. Please be aware that *IN SHAKESPEARE AND THE BIBLE* may not be licensed by Samuel French in your territory. Producers should contact the nearest Samuel French office or licensing partner to verify availability.

For all enquiries regarding Professional productions in the United Kingdom; Professional and Amateur productions throughout the rest of Europe; and motion picture, television, and other media rights, please contact Alan Brodie Representation (Victoria@AlanBrodie.com). Visit www.thorntonwilder.com/contact for details.

No one shall make any changes in this title for the purpose of production. No part of this book may be reproduced, stored in a retrieval system, or transmitted in any form, by any means, now known or yet to be invented, including mechanical, electronic, photocopying, recording, videotaping, or otherwise, without the prior written permission of the publisher. No one shall upload this title, or part of this title, to any social media websites.

MUSIC USE NOTE

Licensees are solely responsible for obtaining formal written permission from copyright owners to use copyrighted music in the performance of this play and are strongly cautioned to do so. If no such permission is obtained by the licensee, then the licensee must use only original music that the licensee owns and controls. Licensees are solely responsible and liable for all music clearances and shall indemnify the copyright owners of the play and their licensing agent, Samuel French, against any costs, expenses, losses and liabilities arising from the use of music by licensees. Please contact the appropriate music licensing authority in your territory for the rights to any incidental music.

IMPORTANT BILLING AND CREDIT REQUIREMENTS

All producers of *IN SHAKESPEARE AND THE BIBLE* must give credit to the author of the play in all programs distributed in connection with performances of the play, and in all instances in which the title of the play appears for the purposes of advertising, publicizing or otherwise exploiting the play and/or a production. The name of the author must appear on a separate line on which no other name appears, immediately following the title and must appear in size of type not less than fifty percent of the size of the title type.

> This play may be performed only in its entirety. No permission can
> be granted for cuttings, readings or any use of parts of the play for
> any purpose whatsoever without the express written permission of the
> Wilder Family LLC. Absolutely *no* changes can be made to the text.

> All producers of *IN SHAKESPEARE AND THE BIBLE* must print the following credit 1/3 of the size of the author's name in the same boldness of type on the initial credits page of all programs distributed in connection with performances of the Play: "This/these [or title of play if more appropriate] became available through the research and editing of F.J. O'Neil."

FOREWORD TO WILDER'S
IN SHAKESPEARE AND THE BIBLE

THE SIN OF WRATH

From the time he began dreaming up plays as a boy Thornton Wilder's vision of the theater transcended conventional boundaries, and to the end of his life his vision continually evolved and expanded. In 1956, he began work on what grew into an extravagantly ambitious project: two cycles of seven one-act plays based on the Deadly Sins and the Ages of Man. *In Shakespeare and the Bible* represents "Wrath" in Wilder's projected cycle on the Seven Deadly Sins.

In what would prove to be his final dramatic works, Wilder sought not only to explore the theatrical possibilities inherent in the Sins and Ages, but (as he phrased it in his private journal on Christmas Day 1960) to "offer each play in the series as representing, also, a different mode of playwriting: Grand Guignol, Chekhov, Noh play, etc., etc." In short, he envisioned nothing less than a *tour de force* of dramatic theme and form encapsulated in the economy and intensity of the one-act play.

Wilder did not complete the challenge he set for himself, but he came close. The surviving work enriches his dramatic legacy and deserves to be remembered as more than a footnote to his lifelong conviction (written soon after *Our Town* opened on Broadway in 1938): "The theater offers to imaginative narration its highest possibilities."

THE SINS AND AGES THEN AND NOW

A brief overview of the history of these plays will help readers place them in Wilder's career as a dramatist. Two Sins, *Bernice* (Pride) and *The Wreck on the 5:25* (Sloth), premiered in English at a special event in Berlin in 1957 (with Wilder performing in *Bernice*). For reasons that have never been clear, for he enjoyed the experience and felt that plays did well, he withdrew them. That same year a third Sin, *The Drunken Sisters* (Gluttony), written as the satyr play for Wilder's full length drama, *The Alcestiad*, proved successful in its premiere on the stage of Zürich's fabled Schauspielhaus.

Five years passed before the continuation of his ambitious scheme appeared on a stage in the United States. In January 1962, two new Ages (*Infancy* and *Childhood*) and a new Sin, *Someone From Assisi* (Lust), opened at Circle in the Square, then located off-Broadway on Bleecker Street, to the reported largest pre-opening advanced sale in that stage's then 11- year history. Billed as "Plays for Bleecker Street," the show of ran for 349 performances.

Then silence. After "Plays for Bleecker Street" closed, no more Sins or Ages appeared. When Thornton Wilder died in 1975 the public record of his 14-play scheme contained only four plays – two Ages (*Infancy* and *Childhood*) and two Sins (Lust and Gluttony).

Today, eleven of Wilder's Sins and Ages are available for production: a completed cycle of the seven Deadly Sins and four of seven Ages of Man. The source of the seven "new" plays is no secret. The missing pieces were found in Thornton Wilder's archives at Yale[1]. From this source, starting in 1995, his literary executor and family released the two plays withdrawn in 1957, *Cement Hands* (Avarice), and four additional titles (*Youth*, *The Rivers Under the Earth* [Middle Age][2], *A Ringing of Doorbells* [Envy] and *In Shakespeare and the Bible* [Wrath]) recovered and completed by the actor, director and friend of Wilder's, F.J. O'Neil. (Mr. O'Neil's valuable notes on the origin of each of these missing links follow the text of each play.)

The public reception of Thornton Wilder's long lost and new plays was gratifying. *The Wreck on the 5:25* was selected as one of the Best American Short Plays of 1994-95. In 1997, the Centenary of the playwright's birth, Kevin Kline starred in a premiere reading in New York of *Cement Hands*, and the works recovered by Mr. O'Neil served as the centerpieces of Actors Theatre of Louisville's 13th Annual Brown-Forman Classics in Context Festival.   Finally, as the capstone to the Centenary celebration, TCG Press in 1997 published the 11 Sins and Ages in Volume I of *The Collected Short Plays of Thornton Wilder*.

---

[1] No additional one-acts remain to be discovered in Thornton Wilder's archives at Yale.

[2] We believe Wilder intended *The Rivers Under the Earth* to represent Middle Age.

Wilder never followed conventional theatrical practice. As a young writer in his "Classic One Act Plays" of 1931, he swept away scenery and played provocative games with time and place. In the Sins and Ages, his farewell as a playwright, he is no less adventurous by way of settings, techniques, stage-craft and themes. One artistic trend of the day especially "fired his imagination" where these plays are concerned: his passionate belief in the value of the arena stage. "The boxed set play," he wrote in 1961, "encourages the anecdote…The unencumbered stage encourages the truth in everyone." Wilder felt so strongly that audiences should be seated as close to the actors as possible that Samuel French, for several years, was only permitted to license these plays to companies agreeing to perform them on a three-sided thrust or arena stage.

***

As part of its celebration of Wilder's one-act plays, Samuel French and the Wilder family take great pleasure in issuing new acting editions for the Sins and Ages long in print and, for the first time, acting editions of the seven new Wilder works. We invite those performing or teaching these plays to visit www.thorntonwilder.com for additional information.

– *Tappan Wilder,*
Literary Executor for Thornton Wilder

CHARACTERS

MARGET, a maid

JOHN LUBBOCK, a young attorney, twenty-seven, Katy Buckingham's
    fiancé

MRS. MOWBREY, Katy Buckingham's aunt, late fifties

KATY BUCKINGHAM, twenty-one

SETTING

An oversumptuous parlor, New York, 1898.

*(All we need see are three chairs, a low sofa and a tab-
oret. Two steps descend from the hall at the back into
the room. A Swedish maid,* **MARGET***, introduces* **JOHN
LUBBOCK***, twenty-seven, self-assured; face and bearing
under absolute control.)*

LUBBOCK. Mrs. Mowbrey wrote me, asking me to call. My
name is Lubbock.

MARGET. Yes, sir. Mrs. Mowbrey is expecting you. She will
be down in a moment, sir. She says I'm to bring you
some port. I'll go and get it.

(Exit **MARGET***.* **LUBBOCK***, hands in his pockets, whistl-
ing under his breath, strolls about examining closely, one
by one, the pictures hanging on the wall invisible to us.*
MARGET *returns bearing a small tray on which are two
decanters and two goblets. She puts them on the taboret.)*

There's port in this one, sir, and sherry in this. Mrs.
Mowbrey says you're to help yourself.

LUBBOCK. Thank you. *(still examining the pictures)* These are
relatives and ancestors of Mrs. Mowbrey?

MARGET. Oh, yes. Mrs. Mowbrey comes of a very fine family.
I've heard her say that that is her father. As you can
see, a clergyman.

LUBBOCK. *(casually)* She lives alone here?

MARGET. Oh, yes. She's a widow, poor lady. And very much
alone. Would you believe it, if I said that no one's
come to the house to call for the whole time I've been
here, except her lawyer man. And, oh yes, the minister
of her church.

LUBBOCK. For several months.

MARGET. Oh, I've been here about a year. But today we're going to have two callers – you, sir, and a young lady that's coming later. Yes, and I mustn't forget when the doorbell rings for the young lady, I'm to take out the decanters before I open the door. Now I mustn't forget that. And then I'm to bring in the tea. Now, you'll help yourself, won't you?

(**MARGET** *goes out.* **LUBBOCK**, *thoughtfully, pours himself a considerable amount of sherry and, sipping it, returns to his examination of the room and the pictures. Enter* **MRS. MOWBREY**, *late fifties, handsome, florid, powdered. She wears a black satin dress covered with bugles and jet. She addresses* **LUBBOCK** *from the hall before descending into the room.*)

MRS. MOWBREY. Mr. Lubbock, I am Mrs. Mowbrey.

LUBBOCK. Good afternoon, ma'am.

MRS. MOWBREY. You don't know who I am?

LUBBOCK. No, ma'am. I got your letter asking me to call.

MRS. MOWBREY. *(coming forward)* Won't you sit down?

(*They sit,* **MRS. MOWBREY** *behind the taboret.*)

Mr. Lubbock, I had two reasons for asking you to call today. In the first place, I wish to engage a lawyer. I thought we might take a look at one another and see if we could work together. (*She pauses. He bows his head slightly and impersonally.*) I mean a lawyer to handle my affairs in general and to advise me. (*same business*) My second reason for asking to see you is that I am your fiancée's aunt.

LUBBOCK. *(amazed)* Miss Buckingham's aunt! She never told me she had an aunt.

MRS. MOWBREY. No, Mr. Lubbock, she wouldn't. I am the black sheep of the family. My name is not mentioned in that house. – Will you pour me some port, please. I am glad to see that you have helped yourself…Thank you…Yes, I am your future mother-in-law's sister.

(*He is standing up, holding his glass – waiting.*)

MRS. MOWBREY. *(cont.)* Our lives took different directions.

(He sits down.)

But before we get into the legal matter, let's get to know one another a little better. – Tell me, I haven't seen my niece for fifteen years. Is she a pretty girl?

LUBBOCK. Yes – very.

MRS. MOWBREY. We're a good-looking family.

LUBBOCK. *(indicating the pictures on the wall)* And a distinguished one. Miss Buckingham would be very interested in seeing these family portraits.

MRS. MOWBREY. Yes. *(she sips her wine, then says dryly, without a smile)* It's not hard to find family portraits, Mr. Lubbock. There are places on Twelfth Street, simply full of them. Bishops and generals – whatever you want.

LUBBOCK. *(continuing to look at them, also without a smile)* Very fine collection, I should say.

(She takes another sip of wine.)

MRS. MOWBREY. Mr. Lubbock, I've made some inquiries about you. You are twenty-seven years old.

LUBBOCK. Yes, I am.

MRS. MOWBREY. You took your time finding yourself, didn't you? All that unpleasantness down in Philadelphia. What happened exactly? Well, we won't go into it. Then you gave yourself a good shaking. You pulled yourself together. Law school – very good. People are still wondering where you got all that spending money. It wasn't horse racing. It wasn't cards. No one could figure it out. Apparently it was something you were doing up in Harlem. – Certainly, your parents couldn't afford to give you anything. In fact, you were very generous to them. You bought them a house on Staten Island. You were a very good son to them and I think you'll make a very good family man.

LUBBOCK. *(with a slight how and a touch of dry irony)* You are very well informed, ma'am.

MRS. MOWBREY. Yes, I am. *(She takes another sip of wine.)* On Saturday nights you often went to 321 West Street "The Palace," you boys called it. Nice girls, everyone of them, especially Dolores.

LUBBOCK. *(mastering violence; rises)* I don't like this conversation, ma'am. I shall ask you to let me take my leave.

MRS. MOWBREY. *(raising her voice)* You and I have met before, Mr. Lubbock. You knew me under another name. I owned The Palace.

LUBBOCK. Mrs. Higgins!!

MRS. MOWBREY. My hair is no longer blond. *(She rises and crosses the room.)* You may leave any moment you wish, but I never believed you were a hypocrite.

LUBBOCK. *(after returning her fixed gaze wrathfully; then sitting down again)* What do you want?

MRS. MOWBREY. Yes, I owned The Palace and several other establishments – refined, very refined in every way. I've sold them. I've retired. I see no one – no one – whom I knew in those days. Except today I am seeing yourself. Naturally, I am never going to mention these matters again. I am going to forget them, and I hope that you will forget them, too. But it would be very valuable to me to have a lawyer who knew them and who was in a position to forget them. – I'll have a little more port, if you'll be so good.

*(**LUBBOCK** takes the glass from her hand in silence, fills it at the taboret and carries it to her. She murmurs: "Thank you." He returns and stands by the taboret, talking to her across the length of the stage.)*

LUBBOCK. I don't believe you asked me here to engage me as your lawyer. There's something else on your mind. will you say it and then let me take my leave?

MRS. MOWBREY. You were always like that, Jack.

LUBBOCK. *(loud)* I will ask you not to call me Jack.

MRS. MOWBREY. *(bowing her head slightly)* That was always your way, Mr. Lubbock. Suspicious. Quick to fight. Imagining that everybody was trying to take advantage of you.

LUBBOCK. What do you want? I don't know what you're talking about. *(he starts with fuming lowered head for the door)* Good afternoon.

MRS. MOWBREY. Mr. Lubbock, I will tell you what I want. *(he pauses with his back to her)* I am a rich woman and I intend to get richer. And I am a lonely woman, and I don't think that that is necessary. I want to live. And when you and Katy are married, I want you to help me. *(he is "caught" and half turns)* I want company. I want to entertain. I also want to help people. I want – so to speak – to adopt some. Not young children, of course, but young men and women who want bringing out in some way or other. I have a gift for that kind of thing. – Even in my former work I was able to do all sorts of things for my girls. – Did you ever hear anyone say that Mrs. Higgins was mean – unkind – to the girls in her place?

(He refuses to answer; the port is going to her head. She strikes her bosom emotionally.)

I'm kind to a fault. I love to see young people happy. Dozens of those girls – I helped them get married. I encouraged them to find good homes. Against my own interest. – Your friend, Dolores married a policeman. Happy as a lark. *(She puts a delicate lace handkerchief to her eyes and then to her nose.)* – Will you consent to be my lawyer?

LUBBOCK. *(scorn and finality)* My firm doesn't allow us to serve family connections.

MRS. MOWBREY. Oh, I don't want to have anything to do with that wretched firm Wilbraham, Clayton, what's-its-name? All you do for me will be on your own time. I shall start giving you three thousand a year for your advice. Then –

LUBBOCK. I beg your pardon. It's entirely out of the question.

MRS. MOWBREY. *(after a slight pause; in a less emotional voice)* Yes, yes. I know that you are always ready with your no! no! You haven't yet heard what I can do for you. And I don't mean in the sense of money. There is something you are greatly in need of… *(pause)* …John Lubbock. One can see that you are a lawyer – and a very good one, I suspect. – So, you looked about you and you selected my niece?

LUBBOCK. Oh, much more than that. I'm very much in love with your niece. You should know her. Katy's an extraordinary girl.

MRS. MOWBREY. Is she? There's nothing very extraordinary about her mother? What's extraordinary about Katy?

LUBBOCK. Why, she's…I feel that I'm the luckiest man in the world.

MRS. MOWBREY. Come now, Mr. Lubbock. You don't have to talk like that to me.

LUBBOCK. *(earnestly)* I assure you, I mean it.

MRS. MOWBREY. *(a touch of contempt)* Very clever, is she? Reads a lot of books and all that kind of thing?

LUBBOCK. No-o. *(with a slight laugh)* But she asks a lot of questions.

MRS. MOWBREY. *(pleased)* Does she? So do I, Mr. Lubbock, as you have noticed. *(She rises and starts toward her former seat by the decanter of port.)* She asks lots of questions. I like that. – I asked her to call this afternoon.

LUBBOCK. *(startled and uneasy)* You did? Did you tell her that I would be here?

MRS. MOWBREY. No. I thought I would surprise her.

LUBBOCK. Katy doesn't like surprises. *(preparing to leave, with hand outstretched)* I think that at your first meeting with – after so long a time – you should see her alone. Perhaps I can call on you at another time.

MRS. MOWBREY. *(still standing)* What are you so nervous about? It's not time for her to come yet, and besides I have this law matter to discuss with you.

LUBBOCK. Thank you. – I'll ask if I can call some other time.

MRS. MOWBREY. Anyway, perhaps she won't come. She'll have shown my letter to her mother and her mother will have forbidden her to come. Would Katy disobey her mother?

LUBBOCK. Yes.

MRS. MOWBREY. *(eyeing him)* Has Katy chosen to marry you against her mother's wishes?

LUBBOCK. Yes. Very much so.

MRS. MOWBREY. I see. Tears? Scenes? Slamming of doors?

LUBBOCK. Yes, I think so.

MRS. MOWBREY. *(leaning toward him confidentially, lifted finger)* Katy is like me, Mr. Lubbock. I can feel it with every word you say.

(Still uneasy, LUBBOCK has been taking a few steps around the room; he looks up at the ceiling and weighs this thoughtfully.)

LUBBOCK. If you told her you were her aunt…Yes, I think she will come. Katy likes to know…where she stands; what it's all about, and that kind of thing.

MRS. MOWBREY. I see. A lawyer's wife. As you suggested a few moments ago: she's inquisitive?

LUBBOCK. *(with a nervous laugh)* Yes, she is.

MRS. MOWBREY. And you think I'm inquisitive, too – don't you?

LUBBOCK. Yes, I do.

MRS. MOWBREY. Well, let me tell you something, Mr. Lubbock. Everybody says we women are inquisitive. Most of us are. We have to be. I wouldn't give a cent for a woman who wasn't. And why? *(The wine has gone to her head. She emphasizes what she is about to say by tapping with jeweled rings on the taboret.)* Because a good deal is asked of us for which we are not prepared. Women have to keep their wits about them to survive at all, Mr. Lubbock. *(She leans back in her chair.)* When I was married I didn't hesitate to read every scrap of paper my husband left lying around the house. But *(She leans forward.)* as I said, I have some business to discuss with you before Katy comes. – Do you always walk about that way?

LUBBOCK. *(surprised)* People tell me I do. I do in court. If it makes you uneasy –

MRS. MOWBREY. I would like to ask another thing. When you are married – and as a wedding present I shall give Katy a very large check, I assure you – I want you both to give me the opportunity to meet some of your friends, young people in whom I could take an interest. New York must be full of them. But most of all I want to see you two. I want you to feel that this house is your second home. *(very emotional)* I will do everything for you. I have no one else in the world. I will do everything for you. *(Again she puts her handkerchief to her face.)* Now I've talked a good deal. Have you anything to say to all this?

LUBBOCK. *(after rising and taking a few steps about)* Mrs. Mowbrey, I like people who talk frankly, as you do, and who go straight to the point. And I'm going to be frank with you. There's one big hitch in what you propose.

MRS. MOWBREY. Hitch?

LUBBOCK. Katy. *(He looks directly at her and repeats.)* Katy. Naturally, she wouldn't have anything to say about my professional life. – And I want to thank you for the confidence you express in my ability to be of service to you. *(He looks up at the ceiling in thought.)* But about those other points I don't know. I tell you frankly, Mrs. Mowbrey, I'm in love with Katy. I'm knocked off my feet by Katy. But I feel that I don't know her. How can I put it? I'm…I'm even afraid of Katy.

MRS. MOWBREY. *(almost outraged)* What? A man like you, afraid of a mere girl!

LUBBOCK. *(short laugh)* Well, perhaps that's going too far; but I swear to you I still can't imagine what it will be like to be married to Katy. *(His manner changes and he goes to her briskly as though to shake her hand.)* Really, I think it's best that I say good night now. Katy will want to see you alone. So I'll thank you very much and say good-bye. And ask if I may call on you at some other time.

MRS. MOWBREY. Nonsense! What possible harm could there be – ? *(the doorbell rings)* There! That's the door-bell. That's Katy. It's too late to go now. Do calm down, Mr. Lubbock.

(enter MARGET*)*

MARGET. That's the front door bell, Mrs. Mowbrey. Shall I take out the tray?

MRS. MOWBREY. Yes, Marget. And be quick about it.

*(*MARGET *scutters out with the tray.)*

Really, I don't understand you, Mr. Lubbock. This is not like you at all. There's nothing to get nervous about. The young girls of today are perfect geese – don't I know them! Pah!

*(*MARGET *at the door)*

MARGET. Miss Buckingham to see you, ma'am.

*(*KATY, *twenty-one, very pretty, stands a moment at the top step and looks all about the room.)*

MRS. MOWBREY. *(throwing her arms wide, without rising)* Ah, there you are, dear.

KATY. *(taking a few steps forward, her eyes on* LUBBOCK*)* Aunt Julia, I'm very glad to see you.

MRS. MOWBREY. *(apparently expecting to be kissed)* This is a joy!

*(*KATY, *approaching her, looks at her smiling, and suddenly drops her reticule which she has opened. Thus avoiding an embrace, she leans over and takes some time picking the objects up.* LUBBOCK *and* MARGET *come to her assistance.)*

KATY. Oh, how awkward of me! I'm so sorry. I'm always doing things like this. Thank you. There's my key… and my card case. Thank you.

MRS. MOWBREY. Marget, we're ready for tea now. I'm sure you'll want some tea, dear.

(*exit* **MARGET**)

KATY. Thank. you, I would. – You're here, John?

LUBBOCK. (*uncomfortable*) Mrs. Mowbrey wrote me and asked me to call.

MRS. MOWBREY. Yes, dear, I've wanted a lawyer so badly. Now sit down and let me look at you.

(**KATY** *sits in the chair* **MRS. MOWBREY** *has indicated.*)

What a dear, beautiful girl you are! – And you're so like my father! You're like me and my father.

LUBBOCK. (*reluctantly*) Yes…There is something there.

MRS. MOWBREY. Oh, I've lost my looks – I know that! I've been through great unhappiness, but the resemblance is there, there's no doubt about it.

KATY. Did you know I was coming, John?

LUBBOCK. No, no.

KATY. Is John going to be your lawyer, Aunt Julia?

MRS. MOWBREY. I hope so, dear. I certainly hope he will be. That'll bring us all closer and closer together.

KATY. Aunt Julia…I scarcely remember you. Why…why haven't we seen you more often?

MRS. MOWBREY. Mildred, dear, your mother and I…let's not talk about it. I'll just say this: sometimes in families, there are people who simply can't get on together. I hope your mother's happy. I wish her every good thing in the world. If she doesn't wish to see me, that doesn't change anything. I wish her every good thing in the world. You can tell her that any time you wish, Mildred. – But Mr. Lubbock tells me you wish to be called Kate?

KATY. Yes, I do.

MRS. MOWBREY. But why?

KATY. *(after looking down a moment)* That would take too long to explain, Aunt Julia.

MRS. MOWBREY. Well, you are a dear original girl, aren't you?

KATY. John, are you Aunt Julia's lawyer?

MRS. MOWBREY. He *will* be. He will be. We've just settled that. So that both my business and my pleasure – my affection, let us hope – will be close together. Oh, here's the tea.

*(enter **MARGET** with the tea service)*

Oh, I have such plans for you. Cream and sugar – both of you?

KATY & LUBBOCK. Thank you.

MRS. MOWBREY. You see, dear, I've lived too much alone, since my dear husband's death. That's not good. That's not right. And you are going to bring me out. – Now tell me, Katy, where are you going to live? Have you found just what you wanted?

KATY. Yes, we have. – Thank you.

MRS. MOWBREY. Splendid! Tell me, dear, don't have a moment's hesitation…What will it be: linen? silver?

KATY. Aunt Julia, I don't like receiving presents. I never have. I may be strange in that, but…I don't.

MRS. MOWBREY. Presents! But I'm your aunt – this is the family.

KATY. *(clearly)* But we don't know one another very well yet.

*(**MRS. MOWBREY** is stopped short. She fumbles with her handkerchief. She begins silently to weep.)*

Have you been living in New York, Aunt Julia?

MRS. MOWBREY. That was not kind, Mildred. That was not kind.

KATY. *(searching herself, softly)* I'm sorry. I'm sorry, if…I think I'm supposed to be a very outspoken person, Aunt Julia, but I didn't mean to be unkind.

MRS. MOWBREY. *(still drying one eye; but in a low firm tone of instruction)* That means you must have been hurt in life, in some way. I've seen it often.

KATY. *(another glance at John, slowly)* No, I...don't think I have.

LUBBOCK. *(floundering, but trying to do his part)* Katy's right, Mrs. Mowbrey. But when she does make a friend, she's a real one.

MRS. MOWBREY. *That* I believe. And so am I. And I want to prove it to you. I want you to come to feel that this is your second home. I want to be useful to you, in any way. Do you know, Katy, that when I was a girl *I* changed my name, too? I was christened Julia; but I didn't like it. I wanted a name out of the Bible. I liked the story of Esther. I liked her courage. That's what I like: courage. Now will you tell me why you changed yours?

KATY. Well...I used to read Shakespeare all the time. And I liked the girls in Shakespeare. Even when I was very young...Every day I'd pretend I was a different one. And, you know, they...most of them have no fathers or mothers, or else...and they have to go live in foreign countries or live in a forest...and they even have to change their clothes and pretend they're men. They're very much thrown on their own resources. That's what they learn. There are four or five that I admired most – but I knew I wouldn't be like them. So I chose one of the lesser ones, one of the easier ones –

MRS. MOWBREY. I remember. I remember. That play. I can't remember its name – but that Kate had an awful temper. Mr. Lubbock, has our Kate got an awful temper?

(KATY stiffens.)

LUBBOCK. No, indeed, Mrs. Mowbrey.

KATY. No, I wish I did. I think people with a temper are lucky.

MRS. MOWBREY. Lucky! How could you wish a thing like that.

KATY. When things seem all wrong to me, I do something worse than have a temper. I turn all cold and stormy inside. It's as though something were dead in me.

MRS. MOWBREY. I understand every word of that. Katy, dear, we will be good friends. – Now surely there's some furniture I can lend you, some household appointments?

KATY. *(quietly)* Thank you very much, Aunt Julia. But, of course, we mean to live very simply. And we won't be seeing anyone for the first year or two. – Will we John?

LUBBOCK. *(floundering)* Just as you wish, Katy...

MRS. MOWBREY. Oh, dear! That's so unwise! My dear children, you must come and see *me* – and my friends. I have so many friends who will be delighted to meet you: artists and writers and young men in politics – so valuable for Mr. Lubbock's work. And the dear rector of my church, Mr. Jenkins.

KATY. All that's for John to decide, of course.

*(**KATY** turns inquiringly toward him, as does **MRS. MOWBREY**.)*

LUBBOCK. *(belatedly he stammers)* Oh, we...won't be seeing too many people...

MRS. MOWBREY. There's Judge Whittaker's son for example. You'll laugh till the tears run down your cheeks. *(with confidential emphasis to **KATY**)* Judge Whittaker can do anything in New York – *anything* you ask him...Old friend of mine. *(to **LUBBOCK**, rising)* People with influence like that – you must know them. *(to **KATY**)* And then I want to take you shopping, dear. Stores where they know me. They practically *give* me the things. Great Heavens, I haven't had to pay the marked [price] for anything, for years. Friends, friends everywhere. – Now I'm going to leave you two alone together. I know you have a world of things to talk about.

*(**KATY** rises.)*

If you want some more tea, just ring and ask Marget for it.

KATY. *(always quietly)* Aunt Julia, I can see John perfectly well in my own home. I came to call on you.

MRS. MOWBREY. *(moving to the door)* What a sweet thing to say. – No, no. I know young people in love; don't say I don't. And beginning today I want you to think of this house as your second home. Besides, I have a present for you and I must go and get it. *(She indicates a ring on her finger.)* A very pretty thing, indeed.

KATY. *(following **MRS. MOWBREY** toward the door; with a touch of firmer protest)* But, Aunt Julia! –

MRS. MOWBREY. Ten minutes! I'll give you ten minutes!

*(She goes out. **KATY** turns and with lowered eyes goes slowly to her chair. She sits and covers her face with her hands.)*

KATY. *(as though to herself)* I can't understand it…What a dreadful, dreadful person.

LUBBOCK. *(uncomfortable)* Come now, Katy. It's not as bad as all that…Of course, she's a little…odd; but I imagine she's been through a lot of…trouble of some sort.

*(**KATY** looks at him a moment and then says with great directness.)*

KATY. What has she done, John? *(He doesn't answer.)* It must be something serious. Mother won't talk about her *one minute!* – Tell me! What is it?

LUBBOCK. Well…uh…she may have made some wrong step…early in life. Something like that.

KATY. *(after weighing this thoughtfully)* No. My mother would have forgiven that…It must be something much worse.

LUBBOCK. Whatever it was it's behind her. It's in the past.

KATY. *(Shakes her head; She gives a shudder.)* It's there – *now.* *(always very sincerely, this as though to herself)* I don't even know the names of things. Except what I've read about. In books. *(brief pause)* *(as with an effort to say such an awful thing)* Was she a…usurer?

LUBBOCK. What's that? – Oh, a usurer. *(with too loud a laugh)* NO, no – she wasn't that!

KATY. Was she a perjurer?

LUBBOCK. Katy, where do you get these old expressions? I don't know, but I guess she wasn't that.

KATY. *(gravely pursuing her thought)* Was she…that other kind of bad person. That word that's in the Bible and in Shakespeare… *(This takes solemn courage.)* …that begins with "double-you"…with "double-you aitch" – ?

(This takes a minute to dawn on LUBBOCK. *He reacts violently; with as little comic effect as possible.)*

LUBBOCK. Katy!! How can you say such a thing.

KATY. I don't know how to pronounce it.

LUBBOCK. Do stop this! Put this all out of your head, *please.*

KATY. But she's my own aunt. I must have some idea to go by. Mother won't say a word. She just bursts into tears and leaves the room.

LUBBOCK. Please, Katy. – For Heaven's sake, change the subject.

KATY. I don't want to know anything that it's *unsuitable* for me to know. But I don't want to live with people hiding things from me. I don't think ignorance helps anybody. I can see perfectly well that you know the answer: Was Aunt Julia that thing that beings with "double-you"?

LUBBOCK. I'm not going to answer you, Katy. This conversation is unsuitable. Very unsuitable.

KATY. *(who has kept her eyes on him; calmly)* Then she *was.*

LUBBOCK. No – I didn't say that. Anyway, how would I know a thing like that? – Probably, she was just connected with such things – at a distance.

KATY. How do you mean?

LUBBOCK. She wasn't in it herself…She just – sort of stood by…I'm not going to stay here another moment. Where's that woman put my hat?

KATY. I see…She arranged them. That's in Shakespeare, too. She was a bawd.

LUBBOCK. Katy!

KATY. It's in the Bible, too: she was a... *(She pronounces the "aitch.")* whoremonger. *(She rises.)*

LUBBOCK. *(fiercely)* Stop this right now. How can you say such ugly words?

KATY. Are there any others that aren't ugly? – Anyway, now I know. *(She quickly moves up toward the entrance.)*

LUBBOCK. Where are you going?

KATY. *(from the steps)* You don't want me to stay, do you?

LUBBOCK. Think a moment, Katy. Stop and think.

KATY. Think what?

LUBBOCK. Well…this Bible you're quoting from…should have taught you to be charitable about people's mistakes. About Mary Magdalene and all that.

KATY. *(turning in deep thought)* Yes, it should, shouldn't it? – But Mary Magdalene wasn't the second thing; she was the first. *(She returns to her chair and sits, her eyes on the floor. Again as though to herself.)* I don't know anything about anything. *(She suddenly looks at him and says with accusing directness.)* And you're not helping me. Tell me what I should think. Are you going to be like this always?…When I ask questions?…

LUBBOCK. *(urgently)* No, Katy. I promise you. I'll answer anything you ask me!

KATY. When?

LUBBOCK. When we're married. – But not here! Not now! – Today, anyway, put all this out of your head.

KATY. *(reluctantly acquiescent, rises again)* When we're married. That's like what Mother's always saying: "When you're older; when you're older." *(turning to him with decision)* But if she *is* those things – those things that Shakespeare said –

LUBBOCK. Don't say them!

KATY. Promise me that you'll never see her again.

LUBBOCK. Now, K-a-a-ty! She's a client. In business we can't stop to take any notice of our client's morals…

KATY. In business they don't? I mean: thieves and criminals? Don't men meet that kind of people all the time?

LUBBOCK. *(putting his hands over his ears)* Questions! Questions! You're going to drive me crazy.

KATY. *(looking around the room, musingly)* And all this money came from…that! *(Her eyes return to him.)* And when she asks us to come here to dinner?

LUBBOCK. Of *course*, we don't have to come often. But she's a lonely woman who's trying to put the mistakes of her life behind her. Be kind, Katy. Be charitable!

KATY. *(weighs this, then says simply)* Have you ever seen her before?

LUBBOCK. Mrs. Mowbrey? *(loud laugh of protest)* Of *course* not.

*(**KATY** goes to the hall. From the top step she turns and says with great quiet but final significance.)*

KATY. And you want me to invite her to the wedding?

*(**LUBBOCK** cannot answer. His jaw is caught rigid. **KATY** returns into the room, drawing a ring off her finger.)*

All I know is what I read in Shakespeare and the Bible. That's all I have to go by, John. Nobody else helps. You don't help me. I'm giving you back your ring.

*(She puts the ring on the taboret and goes quickly, with lowered head, out of the house. The front door is heard closing. **LUBBOCK** stands rigid. Slowly he goes to the taboret and takes up the ring. **MRS. MOWBREY** appears at the hall indignant.)*

MRS. MOWBREY. Who went out the front door? Was that Katy?

(He puts down the ring on the taboret.)

LUBBOCK. Yes, Mrs. Mowbrey. She went home.

MRS. MOWBREY. *(coming in)* Without saying good-bye to me! Her own aunt! Well – there's a badly brought up girl! *(sitting down)* What did she say?

LUBBOCK. She left no message.

MRS. MOWBREY. I'm ashamed of her, Mr. Lubbock. I never heard of such behavior. The idea! *(seeing the ring)* What's this? What's this ring?

LUBBOCK. She left it. It's her engagement ring.

MRS. MOWBREY. She broke her engagement? *(rising)* Mr. Lubbock, listen to me! You can call yourself a very lucky man. One look at her, and I could see she wasn't the right girl for you. – Left without saying one word of good-bye! I don't know what's become of the girls these days. A niece of mine – behaving like that. *(giving him the ring and wagging her finger in his face)* Now you must put that in a safe place – and you'll find the real right girl for you. They aren't all dead yet. You're going to find some splendid girl and I'm going to make a second home for you here. We're going to have fun. *You only live once,* as the Good Book says.

LUBBOCK. *You* did this! Look! *(holding the ring toward her)* She's gone. – You with your conniving and sticking your nose into other people's business. WHY the hell did you have to put your goddamned nose into my affairs?

MRS. MOWBREY. I have never allowed profanity to be used in my presence.

LUBBOCK. Well, you'll hear it now. You – with your sentimental whining about wanting friends. *You'll* never have any friends. You don't deserve to have any friends. God, have you wrecked your chances today! – While you were wrecking mine.

(She has descended coolly into the room. **LUBBOCK** *passes her toward the hall.)*

You can sit here alone for ever and ever, as far as I care. Where'd that girl put my hat?

MRS. MOWBREY. Yes, Mr. Lubbock, you go and you stay away. You have just shown yourself to be the biggest fool I ever saw. It wasn't I that lost you that girl; it was yourself. And you deserve to lose her.

LUBBOCK. How do you know what happened?

MRS. MOWBREY. I will ring and Marget will get your hat. *(She pulls a bell rope. The waiting.)* Katy is my niece. Every inch my niece. She put you to the test and you were… *(vituperatively) Shown up. Shown up.* Oh, you men! On your high saddles.

LUBBOCK. I tried to save you, anyway.

MRS. MOWBREY. I never saw anyone so stupid.

(enter **MARGET***)*

MARGET. Yes, Mrs. Mowbrey.

MRS. MOWBREY. Mr. Lubbock's been looking for his hat, Marget.

MARGET. Yes, ma'am.

*(***MARGET*** disappears and returns with a straw hat.* **LUBBOCK** *takes it.* **MARGET** *disappears.* **LUBBOCK** *lingers at the top of the stairs.)*

LUBBOCK. Well – out with it. What should I have done?

MRS. MOWBREY. In the first place you should have lied, of course. Strong and loud and clear. A girl like that is not ready to learn what she wants to know. And at this stage it's not your business or mine to tell her.

LUBBOCK. She said she left me because I wasn't any help to her. Is lying any help?

MRS. MOWBREY. Of course it is. I suppose you think you were trying to tell her the truth? Young man, you're not old enough to tell the truth and it doesn't look as though you ever will be. In the first place, you should have lied, firmly, cleanly. THEN, you should have shown her that you *were* her friend. Katy did just right. Katy left you standing here, because she saw that you never would be her friend – that you haven't the faintest idea what it is to be a friend. What took place here took place in my own life. It's taking place all the time. Mr. Lubbock, people don't like to be –

*(***LUBBOCK*** rises, crosses the room and says aggressively and a little brutally:)*

LUBBOCK. Mrs. Mowbrey, this has all been very interesting; and you've played your various cards very neatly and all that, but I want to know why you really asked me to come and see you today.

MRS. MOWBREY. *(also getting tougher)* I am coming to that. *(She pauses.)* Do you prefer to stand?

LUBBOCK. *(shortly)* Yes, I do.

MRS. MOWBREY. There's one event in your life – in our lives – that I'd like you to explain to me. One night, at The Palace – it was in the spring of – you lost your head, or rather you lost control of yourself. You broke every bottle in my bar. You did like that with your arm. *(Her arm makes wide sweeping gestures, from right to left and left to right.)* You terrorized everyone. You didn't strike anyone, but the flying glass could have blinded my girls. You weren't drunk. What happened? What made you do that?

LUBBOCK. *(furious, but coldly contained)* I paid for it, didn't I?

MRS. MOWBREY. Oh, Mr. Lubbock. Don't talk like a child. You and I know that there are a great many things that can't be paid for. – Was it something that Dolores said to you – or that I said to you? *(pause)* Or did that friend of yours – what was his name? Jack Wallace or Wallop? – did he hurt your feelings? No, it couldn't be that; because you didn't strike *him.* The only thing you struck was a lot of bottles and *you weren't drunk.*

(She waits in silence; finally he says in barely controlled impatience.)

LUBBOCK. What of it? What of it? I lost my temper, that's all.

MRS. MOWBREY. I can understand your losing your temper at *people,* Mr. Lubbock – we all do; but I can't understand your losing your temper at *things.*

LUBBOCK. What are you trying to get at, ma'am? Out with it. Are you trying to tell me that you think I'm not fit to be the husband of your niece?

MRS. MOWBREY. No, indeed. I think you're just the right husband for her; and the more I talk to you, the more I think you're just the right lawyer for me.

(**LUBBOCK** *is stunned by this sudden shift in* **MRS. MOWBREY**'s *attitude.*)

Now, do you know what I have out in the sun porch? Do you? (*He shakes his head in confusion.*) A bottle of champagne. And do you know what Lena is looking at in the kitchen? Two great big steaks.

LUBBOCK. (*slowly recovering himself*) I don't really like champagne, Mrs. Mowbrey; but would you happen to have any bourbon in the house?

MRS. MOWBREY. Bourbon! Have I bourbon? After six o'clock that's all I touch. (*guiding him to the door*) And if you're a good boy I'll show you the list of my investments. There are one or two I'm worried about. Really worried.

(*She pauses at the top step; he beside her. She puts her hand on his arm.*)

We all have disappointments in life, John – everyone of us – but remember Shakespeare said –

(*She smiles and taps him significantly on the chest with her jeweled forefinger.*)

you know –

(*She laughs and exits. He stands a moment, uncertain, then notices the straw hat still in his hand. He descends into the room, and gazes thoughtfully about. Then he places his straw hat on the taboret, turns and quickly exits in the direction* **MRS. MOWBREY** *has taken. The Lights fade.*)

End of Play

A NOTE ON THE TEXT

The author's manuscript of *In Shakespeare and the Bible* existed in three nearly completed drafts, the latest of which had a number of rewrites, additions and corrections toward a fourth draft. Pages and sections of the earlier drafts, which were lined through or crossed-out, have been examined but have not played a significant part in assembling this version of the play. Wilder's habit of throwing out what he emphatically rejected *("The writer's best friend is his wastepaper basket," is a motto he often articulated),* but keeping around what he might refer to again and use again provided a richly marked road map to the play printed here.

Wilder leaves us wondering whether John will succumb to the strong impulse to grab success at any cost. For this reason I added stage directions [*in brackets*] at the end to give John a moment to collect his thoughts, wonder what the right path is, and then, at least for the moment, to cave in.

F. J. O'Neil
April, 1997

THORNTON WILDER (1897-1975) was an accomplished novelist and playwright whose works explore the connection between the commonplace and the cosmic dimensions of human experience. He won three Pulitzer Prizes: for his novel *The Bridge of San Luis Rey*, and two plays, *Our Town* and *The Skin of Our Teeth*. Wilder's farce, *The Matchmaker*, was adapted as the musical *Hello, Dolly!* He also enjoyed enormous success as a translator, adaptor, actor, librettist and lecturer/teacher. Wilder's many honors include the Gold Medal for Fiction from the American Academy of Arts and Letters and the Presidential Medal of Freedom. Penelope Niven's definitive biography, *Thornton Wilder: A Life*, was published in October 2012. For more information, please visit www.thorntonwilder.com.

Also by
Thornton Wilder...

The Alcestiad

The Beaux' Stratagem (with Ken Ludwig)

The Matchmaker

Our Town

The Skin of Our Teeth

<u>Thornton Wilder One Act Series: The Ages of Man</u>

Infancy

Childhood

Youth

The Rivers Under the Earth

<u>Thornton Wilder One Act Series: Wilder's Classic One Acts</u>

The Long Christmas Dinner

Queens of France

Pullman Car Hiawatha

Love and How to Cure It

Such Things Only Happen in Books

The Happy Journey to Trenton and Camden

<u>Thornton Wilder One Act Series: The Seven Deadly Sins</u>

The Drunken Sisters

Bernice

The Wreck on the 5:25

A Ringing of Doorbells

In Shakespeare and the Bible

Someone From Assisi

Cement Hands

Please visit our website **samuelfrench.com** for complete
descriptions and licensing information.